Reviewers from around the world are talking about the **Wright on Time** books:

Finally! A series of books about children who are learning through living a rich life in a diverse world! Respectful, peaceful parenting, child-led, open source learning and travel all in one book! We're hooked! Maybe the Wrights will travel the world as Nadia and Aidan get a little older and they finish their travels around the US! Imagine if they set off to sail around the world! WooHoo!! The possibilities are endless!!

— Susan Burke

My daughters didn't want me to stop reading. The action, suspense, and sense of adventure kept us turning pages. I was immediately reminded of some of our other favorite learning adventure book series, such as Magic Tree House and The Magic School Bus, in which the characters learn through fun and exciting life experiences.

— Sara McGrath

It's like taking your child on a wondrous road trip across the USA powered by the imagination! You can pick up any book in the series and enjoy it fully without having read others in the series. Of course, if you want to know the complete story of the Wright family's adventures, you are going to want to read the other books!

— Amanda Acuña

How refreshing to read the adventures of a loving family who travel, live, and learn together! All too often parents and children are portrayed in opposition, or parents are simply left out of the

story. The Wright family is a realistic alternative all close families can relate to—whether they travel or not and whether they homeschool or not.

– Elizabeth Holaday

Have you ever dreamed of leaving everything behind, loading the family up in a motorcoach and hitting the road to explore the entire continental US? I surely have! As a homeschooler, that is a huge dream of mine! However, we're not exactly in the place where we can achieve that dream just yet. So, until that time arrives, my family and I will travel along and join in the grand adventures of the Wright family!

– Gina McLeod

This series of books truly took me back to the roots of why we are a homeschool family—the desire to have amazing learning adventures as a family—spending time together everyday—not only with paper and pen, but exploring and learning from the world around us. These amazing books are not only interesting and informative, but wonderfully written and most of all FUN!!

– Jenn Walden

Think the Magic School Bus series of educational chapter books, but for homeschoolers, and much better. Rather than presenting educational facts in 'chunks' or obviously lecture-style explanations, learning opportunities are woven into the dialogue, interests, and discoveries of the characters. As a matter of fact, the very writing style mirrors the philosophies of the delight driven, lifestyle led method of education that the Wrights use to much success with their children.

– Jennifer Bogart

Our curiosity was really piqued by the mysterious device, and we all are anxious to find out more about it. I like the fact that the kids happily befriend adults and love to learn, much like most homeschooled children I know.

— Alicia Bayer

I would highly recommend these books, for homeschoolers and regular schoolers, as they are just wonderful! They are a great length as well, not too long and not too short. We finished the book in a week and that was just perfect for us. My only wish was that I had another one on hand to keep going!

— Heather Preckel

I love the Wright on Time website! I enjoyed reading the FAQ section, and was thrilled to see that you can get lapbooks to go along with the books. This is something that I'm sure other homeschool moms will appreciate as well! If you have visual learners, or you plan on reading these books aloud to your child(ren), then the Flat Kids would be a nice addition. Kids will enjoy the Games page (which includes online puzzles and printable crosswords and word searches).

— Heidi Strawser

The Wright on Time series is a series that writers like me think, "Now, why didn't I think of that?!" I mean, what a concept–an entire series based on each state in the US! Not only is a series like this a writer's dream, it's an awesome collection to build up for children. Homeschooling families need to start getting this series! It teaches some history, a lot of geographical facts, has vocabulary words in the back, and would be great books for book reports! These books are going to be an invaluable resource as time goes on for many families.

— Melissa J from www.mamabzz.com

Lisa has written a truly lovely book. My children and I both learned so much reading about the caves in Arizona, and I have to say it is very nice to have a children's chapter book that is not only fun and educational, but isn't gross. I'm really looking forward to future adventures with the Wright family!

— Alica McKenna-Johnson

While some books that attempt to educate and entertain sacrifice plot and natural dialogue in order to divulge information, Cottrell-Bentley does a superb job of making the discoveries lead to bits of information and the surrounding conversations are both engaging and flow naturally.

— Cheryl Malandrinos

It is always nice to be able to hand my children a book about homeschoolers, children they can relate to. I appreciate this book for that alone, but when you add in the educational value and the enjoyment they derive from this book, you get a winner!

— Elizabeth Dziadul

The children in the book are very likable kids, smart, curious, and well-rounded. Very much like most homeschooled kids I know... In the Wright on Time books, we have great examples of what homeschooling can be like!

— Christine Plaisted

The books were funny and interesting and kept the kids anxious to learn more. I would recommend these books to any homeschooling family—or any family that wants to learn more about the USA. My kids and I can't wait until the next book comes out and read what happens next with the Wright Family!

— Angie Vinez

I love these books because they teach me about the states that I might not have ever visited and known about. I also like these books because they tell about mysteries you have to solve and I love mysteries. I don't want to tell you what the books are about, but there was a part in the first book that made me want to read the second book so that I could solve the mystery. The characters are sort of like me in a way so I relate to them. Because they like mysteries and they like to travel and they love to explore things, just like me. I am looking forward to reading the third book and all the others.

— Kayla, age 10, from Florida

Not only is the book about a family adventure/mystery, there are so many fun facts throughout the book—very educational! In the back of the book, there is a Glossary to refer to as well. It can definitely be used as a fun, home-school resource as well as a supplemental resource for any school children.

— Conny Hutchinson

My 10 year old daughter fell in love. Not only did she love reading about the Wright family's adventures but she also learned about the states they were visiting, which I think was my favorite part. Sure it's fun to read books about vampires and werewolves from time to time, but you're not learning anything. With the Wright on Time book series it's not only a lot of fun, but a great educational experience.

— Joanna Britain

The books are really ideal in that they are really appropriate for a wide age range. Lisa doesn't talk down, or kid-up the language or subjects. I liked how she didn't define and explain every little

educational element like some "educational" chapter books do—
you almost need to go look some things up.

 — Tara Ayers

This series of books is well written, researched and thought
out. It was obvious to me that the author Lisa had experience with
homeschooling, so I was not surprised when I read that both her
children are and always have been homeschooled. Her experience
shines through into her writing as she has included educational
materials at the end of the book to make this series a huge hit
amongst homeschoolers.

 — Kristi Reever

As a mom and homeschooler, I appreciate the educational
aspect of this entire series. Each book is filled with educational facts
about the states as well as vocabulary and reading practice. The
book has a glossary in the back, too, which was a huge plus for this
homeschooler!

 — Angie Knutson

I've really enjoyed these books and I definitely share the love
of learning and traveling around our country. It's exactly what
we've tried to do with our own daughter, even though we don't
have an RV. The series seems to be targeted to readers around
age 10, younger if they love to read and have a parent that likes
to read with them. The stories inspire me to hit the road with
my family!

 — Lynne Peck

…the way the family lives and interacts is a wonderful
example for children; it's not one of those adventure stories

that's packed with all sorts of stuff you wouldn't want your child reading... I love the fact that it's about a homeschooling family; as a homeschooling Mama, I just want to promote, promote, promote this series. ☺

    — Mel from www.mamabzz.com

There's an air of mystery and suspense in the book without being scary to younger children. All the while, they're learning... very similar to the Magic School Bus books, except from a homeschool RV instead of a school bus! This is a chapter book, but the chapters are easy to digest and have little cliffhangers to keep the reader interested. My kids were begging for more.

    — Julie Jackson

My son and I thought this book was FABULOUS! When we first looked to see what the book was about, my son begged me to get it. When it finally arrived he was thrilled! We love the fact that there is a glossary in the back to see what a word means. Plus facts about the state, which is another big plus! Great book for young readers...and they learn so much while reading it! We are anxious for the next book to come out, and I am anxious to keep buying the books for him!

    — Monica Bertone

We also love the fact that there was a glossary in the back, so we were able to find the meanings of a few unfamiliar words. Throughout the book you will experience adventure, as well as humor! I also LOVE how the author includes positive family values which are hard to find in today's children's literature. We highly recommend that you check out this great new series!

    — Stacey Moore

What's amazing is how many facts are unobtrusively set into the storyline... There is also a fairly comprehensive glossary and a state fact sheet at the end of the book... I appreciated the camaraderie demonstrated by the family members—they are real, but they also treat each other with respect.

    — Mozi Esmé

I like that you write the coolest books for kids about REAL life stuff!

    — Shannon Rose

These books are not just for the homeschooled... The fact that the books are a continuation from each other is amazing. The story in itself is superbly written, but the interesting tidbits of information that the reader will gain is so much more. I will be very surprised if you don't find your children researching or taking an interest in the information provided... Don't be surprised if your kids start begging you to homeschool them.

    — Maria Gagliano

Lisa M. Cottrell-Bentley

Wright *on* Time®

WYOMING

Illustrated by Tanja Bauerle

Printed in the United States of America

First Printing, 2010

ISBN: 0-9824829-2-2
ISBN-13: 978-0-9824829-2-6
Library of Congress Control Number: 2010905745

Do Life Right, Inc.
P.O. Box 61
Sahuarita, AZ 85629

Visit www.WrightOnTimeBooks.com to order additional copies or
e-mail sales@wrightontimebooks.com to inquire about bulk discounts.

To my loving husband
Greg
who continues to stick with me through thick and thin

WYOMING

Wyoming became a State on July 10th, 1890

Cutthroat Trout
State Fish

Yellowstone
National Park

Cody

Grand Teton
National Park

Jade
State Gemstone

Jackson

Buffalo
State Mammal

Gannett Peak
13,802 ft.

Rock
Springs

The Equality State
State Nickname

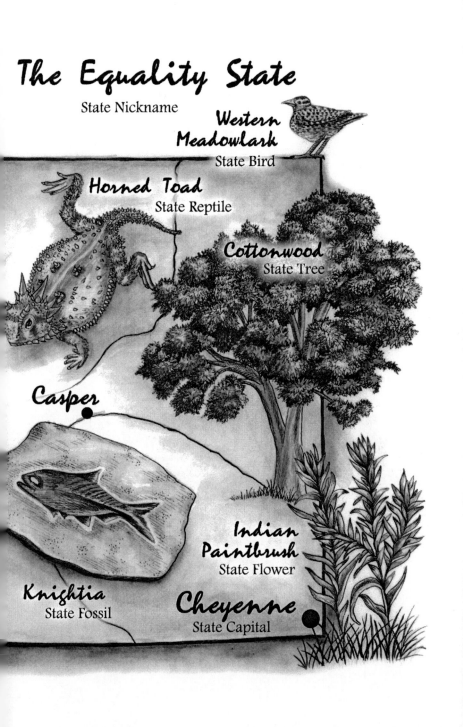

Western Meadowlark
State Bird

Horned Toad
State Reptile

Cottonwood
State Tree

Casper

Indian Paintbrush
State Flower

Knightia
State Fossil

Cheyenne
State Capital

Chapter One

"**H**i, Grandpa! Hi, Grandma!"

"Hi, Nadia," the two grandparents said at the same time. They recognized their eleven-year-old granddaughter's voice instantly on the phone.

"So, where are you now?" Grandpa asked.

"Have you reached South Dakota yet? The badlands are certainly lovely," Grandma said, as she looked out her car window approvingly.

"Nope. We're still in Wyoming. I know we're supposed to meet at Mount Rushmore this week, but it doesn't look like that's going to happen."

"Where are you in Wyoming?" Grandma asked.

"We're at the same campground right by Yellowstone," Nadia replied.

"You haven't left yet?" Grandpa asked, surprised at the news.

"Nope. The mechanic says it'll be at least another week before they find the part for our engine, but Dad doesn't believe it. He told us it will probably be two or more weeks, with delivery," Nadia explained.

"What happened exactly?" Grandma asked, sounding a bit worried.

"Well, we had been camping and sightseeing all around Yellowstone National Park," Nadia started the story. "Oh! By the way, Old Faithful is really cool, but a lot of the park stinks like rotten eggs! On our last day here, we noticed a problem with our RV."

"How long were you planning on staying?" Grandma asked.

"Three days. It's now been a week and three days, but it looks like it might be a *month* and three days!" Nadia exclaimed. Her disappointment at not seeing her grandparents was showing through.

"What's the problem exactly?" Grandpa asked calmly. He was a retired airplane engine mechanic, so he knew all about motors.

WYOMING

"We weren't sure at first. The RV just wouldn't start. So, after Dad fiddled around a bit with it, eventually he called the dealership. They found us a local mechanic who, after a few days, was able to come to our campground to check things out."

"And?" Grandma interjected.

"They said something must have chewed on some cords. Plus, something was added into the engine itself. They've taken it apart and believe it was carried by a rodent or something. Litter or something. It's really messed things up. We think it was probably a water vole since we're right by a stream."

"But, you're all okay?" Grandma clarified. She was always the worrier. It was hard on her when she found out her daughter and her family were planning to travel around the country for a year or more. She was used to seeing them at least once a week and was beginning to miss them terribly.

"We're fine, Grandma. No need to worry." Nadia smiled to herself. It felt good to hear her grandma cared so much, especially because Nadia cared so much for them.

"So, what are the plans now then?" Grandpa asked.

"We're not sure when we are leaving. We're just going to hang out here for a while, I guess. Dad's missed his deadline for the South Dakota Black Hills vacation article, but he's working on an alternative fuel vehicles article now, so he is able to write. Mom has been able to log on to her wireless service from wherever we've been, so she is still working."

Harrison, Nadia's dad, was a freelance writer. Stephanie, her mom, was a telecommuting computer programmer. Their flexible jobs, as well as the fact the children were homeschooled, allowed them to travel freely and live in their recreational vehicle.

"And how are you and Aidan doing?" Grandma asked with real concern in her voice.

Nadia tried to be upbeat. "We're fine. Mostly swimming and hiking. It's been really fun. It took some finagling," she used Grandma's words when she talked with her, "to get an extended open-ended reservation here though. Apparently it's high season and the campground has been booked for months. We can only stay a few more days before we'll have to get the RV towed. I can't imagine what will tow our huge RV or where we'll stay if they do." Nadia couldn't help but sound worried.

"I'm sure your mom and dad will take care of everything and find a great place for all of you to stay," Grandpa reassured her.

WYOMING

"I know, I know. I'm just disappointed we won't be seeing you," Nadia admitted.

The Wright family had planned on being in South Dakota at the same time as Nadia and Aidan's grandparents. They'd been on the road driving through Arizona, Utah, and Wyoming for two and a half months now, and were looking forward to their long-awaited visit.

"So, your traveling plans are up in the air?" Grandma asked.

"Dad says as soon as the engine is fixed we'll be driving straight through until we catch up to where we are supposed to be. So, they're not completely up in the air. It just feels that way," Nadia said slowly.

"Let *me* talk!" Seven-year-old Aidan was simply not able to be quiet anymore.

"Hey, get your own computer," Nadia said to Aidan as she tried to hold the computer for her own use.

Nadia was talking to Grandpa and Grandma over VoIP, otherwise known as Voice over IP or Voice over Internet Protocol. It made it possible for the Wright family to have telephone, texting or video calls to anyone in the world with a telephone or computer. Grandpa and Grandma were using mobile phones for their end of the call, so this call was voice only.

Wright ✸n Time®

"Mom's working and we only have two computers. This isn't home, you know, where we each have our own computer."

Aidan tried to squeeze next to Nadia, nearly knocking her out of the seat. His curly hair and head covered the screen, making it impossible for Nadia to see it.

"Hey!" Nadia hollered, trying to move him back out of the way.

"It's *my* turn! You've been talking too long," Aidan insisted, as he wriggled behind her.

"But, I haven't even told them about the device yet!" Nadia protested, trying to hold her position in front.

"Is that all you can think about?" he asked her, wiggling himself next to Nadia, front and center.

"Hey!" Nadia threw off the headset, stood up, and rushed toward the bedroom. "Mom! Aidan won't let me finish using the computer to talk to Grandpa and Grandma!"

Stephanie looked up from her programming and blinked. She'd been in-the-zone and hadn't heard a single thing Nadia had said.

"Did you hear me?" Nadia asked.

"What?" Stephanie said. "Uh, no. Sorry, honey, I guess I didn't hear you. I was concentrating on getting done with this debugging."

WYOMING

Nadia stood there with her arms crossed, hips cocked, and red hair mussed from whipping it wildly back and forth as she spoke. Her lips were pouty and pursed, ready to yell again.

Stephanie had been sitting at her make-shift desk at the head of the bed. She set her laptop aside, scooted nearer to Nadia, and then sat on the end of the bed so she could give Nadia her full attention.

"What seems to be the problem?" Stephanie asked calmly.

"*Aidan* is taking over the computer space and won't let *me* talk to Grandpa and Grandma *anymore*," she blurted, angrily.

Stephanie paused, making sure Nadia didn't have anything more to say. "Had you been talking for a long time?" she asked, trying to find out more information.

"No, I'd barely *even started* and he practically pushed me out of the chair! I barely got to say *anything* to them!"

Stephanie took a deep breath. She knew it was important to keep calm when her children were worked up. "You seem upset."

"Uh, yeah." Nadia's eyebrows rose as she looked at her mom.

"Aidan pushed you out of your chair and took the headset from you so you couldn't finish talking with your grandparents?"

"More like, couldn't start!"

"He actually pushed you?"

"Well, not *actually*, but he was wiggling all around my seat and getting in my way!"

"Okay. Did he actually take the headset off your head?" Stephanie asked, not taking her kind eyes off of Nadia's.

"Well, no... I actually threw it at him since he wouldn't shut up about wanting to use the computer." Nadia stomped her right foot and re-crossed her arms. Her long red hair was swinging again.

"You definitely sound angry."

"It's because I am!" Nadia screamed. "Can you just let me talk with them more?"

"Yes. Definitely. I'm almost finished with what I was working on. Just give me one minute to save what I was in the middle of, and then you can use my laptop."

"Fine," Nadia said, trying not to look too pleased with her mom's kind offer.

"Will that be acceptable?"

WYOMING

"Fine. I was just in the middle of some things on that computer." She pointed toward the living area where their second laptop sat on the table, with Aidan sitting in front of it, giggling loudly with their grandparents. "I was looking up the properties of the metals Maeve's metallurgist friend e-mailed me about." Maeve was a linguist friend who had been helping Nadia and Harrison decipher the many codes on their mysterious device.

Living in an RV full-time was starting to feel cramped and claustrophobic after over two months on the road. All of the Wrights were missing their belongings, their friends, and their private rooms at home. On top of everything, Stephanie knew the children were starting to get impatient and bored with swimming and hiking in the same place every day.

Stephanie did some quick thinking. "I have an idea," she said to Nadia. "Just give me a minute."

Stephanie scooted back to her lap desk at the head of the bed where her laptop was placed. She typed for a minute, put her own headset on, and then started talking into her mouthpiece. Nadia stood still, watching and waiting.

"Harrison, hi. Where are you?" Stephanie said. "I see. Can you get home sooner?"

"This isn't home," Nadia murmured under her breath.

Stephanie continued her one-sided conversation. "No, I think you need to come home, and then go back there again with the kids."

She paused.

"Or, at least with Aidan."

She paused again.

"Yes, that's exactly it."

She paused again.

"No, they'll love it."

She paused again.

"Yep, see you in a bit then."

Stephanie clicked a few buttons with her touchpad mouse, then said, "Hello? Can you hear me?"

Nadia wondered who her mother was talking to now.

"Hi, Mom. Hi, Dad." Stephanie smiled as she heard her parents' voices. They seemed so far away, but their voices were as crisp and clear as if they were standing right next to her. "Aidan, are you on the phone still?"

Nadia heard Aidan from the other room and knew he was still talking with their grandparents. She was calmer now and sat on the end of the bed. She half-listened to everyone talking in the background while she waited until she could use a computer again. She plopped back and closed her eyes. The next thing she knew, Aidan

WYOMING

was handing the headset back to her while her mom was setting the laptop Nadia had been using next to her.

"Guess I must have dozed," Nadia said as she sat up.

"Sorry for pushing you in the chair," Aidan said. "I just wanted to talk to them, too."

Nadia was calm now. "I know, it's all right. I'm sorry for yelling at you and not offering you a turn. I just really wanted to tell them a couple of things first," she said. "I just miss them and... well, *everything* and I'm tired of being cooped up here."

"Me, too," Aidan said.

"Grandpa and Grandma are still on the phone if you want to talk," Stephanie said to Nadia.

"I do." Nadia quickly put the headset back on, flipped onto her belly, kicked her feet up and started talking into the headset. "So, where was I?" she asked her grandparents. "Have I told you about the strange device we found in the caves of Arizona?"

Chapter Two

Aidan and Nadia's dad, Harrison, pulled their little silver electric car into the parking area alongside their RV and plugged the car into its electrical socket. His jet black hair was plastered down on his head from sweat. There was no wind on this hot July day and their car's air conditioning system wasn't working very well.

Stephanie stepped out of the RV as she heard Harrison driving up.

"Hi," she said. "Hot enough for you?"

Wright 🐢n Time®

A Wyoming summer didn't compare to an Arizona one, but with the work he'd been doing and the long sleeves he was wearing, Harrison was hot. They'd learned the sun was deceptive at high altitudes. Even when it seemed cool to the Arizonans, they could still get sunburned.

Harrison laughed. He was often able to keep his sense of humor, even when the circumstances didn't warrant it. His light-hearted nature helped make the family feel relaxed, especially when things weren't going according to plan.

"I'm fantastic." He smiled at his wife and showed off his grease covered hands and clothing. "I didn't have time to completely clean up."

"How is the mechanic's shop research coming?"

"Good." He took the towel and cleaner Stephanie was holding out for him.

"Thanks for taking the kids with you this afternoon. They're curious about the engine work, and they are bored around here. There are just so many acorns and pinecones they can collect. Only so many tadpoles they can watch. Only so many handstands they can do in the pool."

"Yeah, that's about what I was figuring," he said as he finished wiping his hands.

WYOMING

Stephanie's brows were furrowed. "I'll probably come too."

"Don't worry," Harrison said. "The whole trip won't be as hard as this past week has been. I promise."

She looked up at him, smiling and squinting in the hot sun. "Well, you did say this would be an adventure."

The two hugged and then laughed as they entered their RV home.

Harrison bellowed, "Prince Pumpkin the Third, I'm home." He was mimicking Aidan's most frequent "I'm home" greeting. His hands clean now, he went over to the turtle's terrarium and opened it. He bent down and stroked the turtle's little head. Prince Pumpkin the Third stretched his neck out and Harrison stroked it obligingly. "Did anyone feed this fellow this morning?" he asked Stephanie.

Aidan was off the phone by then. "I did, but I bet he wouldn't mind another pea or two."

"I bet you're right." Harrison opened the fridge and got the little turtle a snack. He then proceeded to make a plate of different nuts, fruits, veggies, hummus, and crackers for the rest of them to eat for lunch. He made sure to add plenty of crushed peppers to his plate.

"So, are the new cables here yet?" Nadia asked as she joined them, grabbing some grapes off the plate.

"Yes! The cables are in, but the engine parts still aren't."

"No moles, voles, trolls or whatever in sight? Our RV doesn't need anymore holes!" Aidan said as he stuffed his mouth with a hummus covered baby carrot. He was certain another animal would chew the new cables before they'd even had a chance to be installed.

"No worries," Harrison said. "I have a surprise though."

"What?" the other three asked simultaneously.

"An alternative energy specialist from Casper is meeting us this afternoon. He's going to be helping me with my article, and he offered to take us all on a tour of a couple of different alternative energy locations today."

Nadia looked sullen and just stared at her father. Aidan leapt up for joy. Stephanie looked a bit grim as she looked into her husband's eyes.

"It'll be fun! I promise," Harrison said with his most convincing voice as he looked back at the two of them across the table. Then the three of them looked back skeptically at Aidan, while he jumped around as though he was just invited to go to a private tour of the reptile cages at the zoo.

WYOMING

Their little silver electric car was charged and ready to go. After lunch, the Wright family started driving back to Yellowstone National Park. They'd spent many hours there during their extended stay and yet they still had only seen a small portion of the extremely large park.

"We're meeting Bert Hendricks, the specialist I was telling you about, at a geyser," Harrison said.

"Old Faithful?" Aidan asked.

"Castle?" Nadia asked.

"Riverside?" Stephanie asked as she listed another of the famous geysers in the park.

"Not any of those," Harrison said with a smile on his face. His family was interested and happy again, and he was very happy to see it.

"Grand?" Nadia guessed again.

Harrison shook his head.

"Echinus?" Stephanie asked.

"It must be Dragon's Mouth! That one was my favorite. That flicking tongue of water was freaky cool," Aidan exclaimed.

"No, you'll never guess. It's a small unnamed one that's near Firehole River."

"Unnamed?" Nadia asked, surprised. She was definitely interested now.

"Yes," Harrison continued as they entered the park and showed the Ranger their yearly National Parks pass. "Believe it or not, there are hundreds of geysers in Yellowstone Park. In fact, there are more than ten thousand hydrothermal features here. Plus, this park contains half of all of the entire world's geothermal features."

"Wow!" Aidan said. "Freaky cool!"

"What are the other hydrothermal, or was that geothermal, features?" Nadia asked.

"What do those words even mean?" Aidan asked.

Stephanie answered. "Geo means *earth*. Hydro means *water*. Thermal means *heat*."

"So geothermal means *earth-heat*..." Nadia began.

"And hydrothermal means *water-heat*," Aidan interrupted, happily now understanding the new scientific words.

"Right," said Stephanie.

"So, what are the other kinds of geothermal features, Dad?" Nadia asked again.

Harrison worked his way to the meeting spot as he tried to remember all the different features this park had. He'd just read about them, so he hoped he wouldn't forget one. "Let's see... Well, there are hot springs, mudpots, and fumaroles."

WYOMING

"Fume-a-Rolls?" Aidan asked. "Sounds like food for a fire-breathing dragon. Yum… and it's making me hungry again."

"We just ate. How can you be hungry again already?" Nadia asked.

Aidan just shrugged his shoulders.

"Fumaroles are actually steam vents," Harrison continued, ignoring Aidan's ongoing request for food.

"Like from a volcano?" Nadia asked.

"Exactly like from a volcano! In fact, pretty much the whole of Yellowstone National Forest is in the crater of an extinct volcano called a *caldera*," Harrison said.

"How amazing is that?" Nadia announced.

"Pretty amazing," her dad replied.

"It's the hot springs that sound nice to me. I'd like to just sit back and relax in one," Stephanie said.

"Dad, what was the other word you said? Something about a pot of mud? Didn't we see those the other day?" Aidan asked.

"Mudpots," Nadia corrected. "Those are the stinky, bubbly, muddy things we saw. Gross," Nadia remembered.

"Hot springs and mud baths? Oh, it's just like a spa," Stephanie joked, with a hint of longing in her voice.

"Of course, not quite as pleasant smelling as a spa though," Harrison joked back. "They are not as safe either. Some of those water features have boiling water. We *really* don't want to go into those!" Harrison said.

"Do we still have the brochures we got the first day we were here, or did you recycle them?" Nadia asked.

"They're in the glove compartment," Harrison replied.

Stephanie got them out and handed them to Nadia. Nadia started scouring through them, seeing if there was more information about the giant caldera.

The Wright family drove up to the unnamed geyser and parked. A middle aged man was sitting cross-legged on the ground near the edge of the water. He was wearing a Forest Ranger type hat, sunglasses, a bright red shirt, and hiking apparel.

"Howdy, Wright Family!" the man hollered as he saw Harrison step out of the car.

"Hi! You must be Bert. It's so nice to meet you. I'm Harrison." Harrison went up to the man and shook his hand.

Bert hopped up, unfolding his tall thin frame. His moves appeared effortless as he stood at least a head taller than the already tall Harrison.

WYOMING

Nadia scanned him from top to feet and back again. "Wow, you're tall!"

"Really freaky tall!" Aidan joined them.

"Hi, I'm Stephanie and these are our observant children, Aidan and Nadia," Stephanie said with a little laugh.

"Nice to meet you all," Bert said with a grin. He looked to the children. "I am tall, aren't I? They used to call me Red, and not just because my hair used to be red, but because I was as tall as a redwood tree on the court."

"The court?" Aidan asked.

"Before I got into alternative energies, I was a professional basketball player, Robert 'Red' Hendricks, number 42. I like to be called Bert nowadays though. In fact, my basketball career is how I can afford to have so many experiments today. I invested some of my money into my own alternative energies business, among other things."

"Freaky awesome! I love basketball!" Aidan exclaimed as he continued to admire the height of his new friend.

"Freaky is a word my son uses for really cool things," Stephanie chimed in with an apologetic tone.

"Freaky awesome word," Bert smiled at Aidan. "I always like to learn the latest slang."

"If you don't mind my asking, just how tall are you?" Nadia asked.

"I'm six foot eleven and a half, and I wasn't even close to being the tallest guy on any of my teams except in high school."

"Wow," Stephanie said as she looked up at him. She hadn't felt short in a long time, but Bert's height made just about everyone feel tiny.

"Let's get started," Harrison said, changing the subject. "As you already know from our talk on the phone, our RV has two gas tanks. One for biodiesel and one for regular diesel when we can't get local biodiesel, but that hasn't happened yet. Plus, our car here runs from an electric motor. So, we're really interested in lots of different renewable energy sources."

"Alrighty then. Let me show you what might just be… the next main energy source for our world," Bert said as he led the way with long strides.

It was a small hike to the secluded area. The Wright family were not sure what they would find, so they kept a careful lookout for anything that might be what Bert was talking about as they walked along the path.

Chapter Three

"**H**ere it is! This is *Lil' Petite*, my favorite geyser in the whole wide world," Bert said. "I like to call it *Lil' Petite,* since it's so small and yet so brilliant. This is an unofficial name, of course. Lil' Petite is filled with minerals and color. Look!" Bert pointed toward a little round crater in the middle of the stream. The stream was a tributary to the Firehole River. "You can see how it's prismatic too."

"It is awesome," Nadia said.

"Freaky awesome!" Aidan said. "But, what's prismatic mean?"

"You know, it means it's like a prism. Like a rainbow." Nadia paused. "Wow, look at all the colors! It's amazing." she said.

"It almost looks like one of those window light-catchers, you know those crystals that hang in Grandma's kitchen window? But it's not see-through like those. Where do all the colors come from?" Aidan asked.

"Could it be all the minerals in the soil?" Harrison guessed as he looked at Bert.

Stephanie got out her camera and took several photographs. She repositioned herself, trying to capture the perfect angle on the beautiful colors.

"Actually, if you look closely, you can see steam on the top of the water. It's the water vapor and the sun together causing a prism effect," Bert said. "It's also a clue to help us with an alternative energy source."

Nadia and Aidan bent down low like their mom already was and examined it from the side.

"I see it! There's steam right above the water," Aidan said, fascinated by the geyser's secrets.

"So what does this have to do with alternative energy?" Nadia asked as she stood back upright.

"I'm glad you asked," Bert said. "I have learned quite a bit about all of this because it has really become my

WYOMING

passion to find a replacement for fossil fuels. With your electric car and biodiesel RV, I'm sure you'll appreciate the possibility of geothermal energy sources."

"Does that mean earth-heat?" Aidan asked, trying to remember what was said before.

"You're a bright kid!" Bert said. "Yep, geothermal means anything pertaining to the heat from the earth. The amazing thing is that we have figured out how to actually harness that heat and turn it into energy for people to power their houses and cars and anything else we might want to use the energy for. It can also heat water and homes directly, without having to turn it into a common-use energy, so you can definitely see how it's a great natural resource."

"You're not talking about putting power companies here, are you?" Stephanie asked, thinking about how beautiful the park was and what it would look like to have a power company sitting on top of this amazing site.

"No, not here. We don't want to mess up the few geysers left in this world. They are a very rare occurrence. Geothermal energy, on the other hand, exists everywhere on Earth."

"Everywhere on Earth?" Nadia asked.

"Yes, Yellowstone National Park is just a convenient place to really see it in action because the heat is so close to the surface. Anyone with a bit of land, even just half an acre or so, could dig their own geothermal well, essentially, and use the power from it to generate electricity for their home. 'The Geysers' is a power field in California with many different power plants that utilize the steam from fumaroles."

"There's that word again. It reminds me of *furcula*," Aidan noted.

"I was thinking the same thing, Aidan," Nadia said. She explained to Bert about their adventure in Utah where they helped to uncover an Allosaurus fragilis' furcula, or wish bone. He was obviously impressed.

"Dinosaur fossils are amazing, aren't they? You know, the petroleum which most cars use today is a kind of fossil fuel called crude oil. Other fossil fuels are coal and natural gas. We call it a *fossil* fuel because it was created from the preserved remains of prehistoric algae and zooplankton," Bert said.

"Yes, I know. Isn't that interesting?" Nadia said.

"Yes, it is. Remember all those oil derricks we saw in Eastern Utah?" Harrison asked the kids.

Nadia and Aidan nodded.

"Well, they were pulling up crude oil from the earth."

"Couldn't they find any polite oil?" Aidan joked.

"Not that kind of crude." Bert smiled. "It means raw, unrefined. There are huge oil-shale and tar-sand reserves there in Utah. However, hydrocarbons, the main compounds that make up fossil fuels, are not renewable. Which is why my company concentrates on other sources of energy," Bert said.

"What do you mean by renewable? You mean you can check it out of the library?" Aidan asked.

"Renewable means we can keep making more of it all the time, unlike fossil fuels which took millions of years to make. Our modern world has almost used them up in just a couple of hundred years. Renewable energies are made much more quickly. There are many choices of these renewable energies that could help us replace fossil fuels within your lifetime," Bert said.

"Like what?" Nadia was curious now.

"Geothermal, of course, is one of my favorite renewable energies. Added to that list are solar, wind, and biofuels, like the biodiesel your RV uses. Oh, and of course hydroelectric, but my company doesn't work with that source currently. There's also biomass, tidal, wave, nuclear fission and fusion, and physical energy powers. Some of them are even confidential at this point for patenting reasons. We are all trying to figure out what will be the next main energy source. It's still undecided, and it just might be a combination of things..." Bert turned to look at Lil' Petite again, "and then there's water."

"Oh, I love the idea of a top-secret renewable energy source! That's totally freaky cool!" Aidan said.

"What do you mean by water?" Nadia asked.

"Here is a mystery for you..." Bert said. "What energy source are we going to explore next?"

Just then, Lil' Petite spouted water ten feet into the air. The water sputtered a bit and sprayed a furious, small spray. The Wrights were silenced by the wonder of the geyser.

After a minute, Lil' Petite stopped.

Nadia started to ask another question, when it spat again. Little spits of water flew into the air. It looked just liked Old Faithful's *little* sister. Bert had picked the perfect name for this officially unnamed geyser.

"That is freaky awesome!" Aidan declared once the geyser had completely stopped.

"I couldn't agree more," Bert said.

Chapter Four

"This is it," Bert finally said an hour and a half later after they'd been traveling in the Wright's car.

The Wrights looked out the car window and saw a big building alongside a winding river.

"It's a hydroelectric water plant. There are quite a few hydroelectric plants in the United States. There's a big one at the Flaming Gorge Dam in the southwestern part of Wyoming. You've also probably heard of the big one south of Niagara Falls. The electricity generated from that plant goes all the way to New York City."

Wright ✴ n Time®

The four Wrights tumbled out of the little silver car, while Bert squeezed out carefully. Bert had to unfold his tall body frame so he wouldn't hit his head. The car wasn't made for comfort, but efficiency, so his tall frame only fit inside with a lot of folding like origami.

"How much charge is left in your car?" Bert asked, concerned they might be stranded if the car didn't have much battery life left in it since they'd been driving for so long. "I think there is an electric car hook-up here if you want to park closer to the building."

"Oh, we're fine for quite a while, at least another two hundred miles. I charged it to its max earlier this morning," Harrison said. "No worries." One of the problems of early electric cars was that they had to be recharged very frequently. It made driving long distances a problem. The Wrights' prototype electric car didn't have that issue.

"I had no idea a power plant could be so pretty," Stephanie said as she started toward the river to get some close up photographs of the area.

"How long has water been used to make power?" Nadia asked.

"Oh, a long time," Bert said. "Think of old fashioned water wheels. They were a form of harnessing water energy."

"I've never seen one of those," Aidan said.

WYOMING

"Neither have I," Nadia said, "except in photographs."

"It sounds like we're going to have to find one on our trip! I think I might already know where one is," Harrison said.

Bert went back into excitement mode. "The really great thing about hydropower, that's energy from water..."

"Because hydro means water," Aidan piped in.

"Exactly. The really great thing about hydropower is that it's a clean, carbon-free, renewable energy. If only we could get all of our electricity this way!"

"What do you mean by carbon-free?" Aidan asked.

"Remember when I told you about hydrocarbons being the main compounds of fossil fuels? Well, *hydrocarbons* are made from hydrogen and carbon elements put together. Carbon-free energies are sources made without fossil fuels. They also don't produce any gases like carbon monoxide and carbon dioxide which can hurt the environment."

"Oh, so the rude oil from the prehistoric algae and the plankton from zoos is a carbon fuel?" Aidan asked.

"That's *crude* oil, not rude oil!" Nadia laughed.

"And the plankton isn't from zoos, it's zo-o-plankton," Stephanie said.

"Oh, yeah... right!" Aidan laughed along. "So, the crude oil is a carbon fuel?"

"Exactly." Bert smiled at the fun the kids were having. "All living things are carbon based. Carbon is an element found in all life forms."

"Freaky cool!" Aidan said. "I'm totally going to have to tell Connor about this!" Connor was Aidan's best friend from Arizona, who was now his daily pen-pal thanks to e-mail.

They walked as close as they could to the hydroelectric power plant. The mist in the air had been cooling them nicely, so Nadia was starting to get cold. She decided to go back to the car to grab her jacket.

* * *

Nadia put her pink windbreaker over her head and zipped up the little top zipper. She loved how the jacket was the exact same shade as a summer sunset. People always made comments whenever she wore it. She fiddled with the front kangaroo pocket and felt the smooth surface of their mystery device.

She thought about the glow which came from within the Time Tuner and she wondered what alternative energies *it* must be using. She quickly ran back to the group. She just had to talk to Bert about what he thought was giving the device its power… and why. As she walked toward the power plant, the Time Tuner began to glow in her pocket.

Chapter Five

"Wind and water are often found in close proximity," Bert was saying as Nadia rejoined the group.

Bert opened a side door to the facility, and they all entered it. He briefly talked to a woman who was sitting and typing behind a small desk. She seemed to know him and nodded as they spoke. Bert came back and explained that their group was allowed to walk around with him as their guide. Nadia soon became interested in the details of the facility and forgot to mention the Time Tuner to Bert.

Wright ☙n Time®

"What are all of these control panels and levers?" Nadia asked once they were past the desk area.

"A power plant like this doesn't completely run itself," he said with a smile. "It takes a lot of people and equipment for the operations to work smoothly. Modern day hydroelectric power plants are a lot more involved than water wheels, but the concept is basically the same."

They walked through the entire plant as Bert spoke excitedly about the possibilities of the carbon-free energy source of hydro-power. After the inside tour, they stood outside and watched the plant in action from the side of the river. Birds could be heard singing in the distance while the sound of the wind through the trees mingled with the sounds of water running.

"Why is so much water being held back?" Aidan asked.

"That's what dams are for," Stephanie explained. "The water is held in order to control the flow better. The excess water collected is being held in a reservoir, which is just a big container for water."

"Aren't beavers the ones who usually make dams?" Aidan giggled.

"Yes," his mom smiled back. "It's probably where humans got the idea."

"Are there lots of places like this?" Nadia asked. "I don't remember seeing any in Arizona."

WYOMING

"There's actually a really big dam on the border of Arizona and Nevada with the Colorado River. That's the Hoover Dam. We will have to think about stopping there on the way home," Harrison said. "But, it's true. There are no hydroelectric power plants near Tucson. That's where we're from," Harrison commented to Bert.

"But, there are a lot of solar and wind generators in Arizona. It's the ideal environment for those," Bert said.

"How do they decide where to put a water one?" Nadia asked.

"A dam is best placed where there is a big drop in elevation of a river. You know, where there's a river on a big hill and there is a nice strong supply of water," Bert said. "Niagara Falls is a very dramatic example of a drop in a river. There they divert part of the water through underground conduits, or pipes, to turbines. The hydroelectric plant there produces energy for New York."

"So how exactly does this water produce electricity?" Nadia asked Bert.

"Yeah, and how is the power stored? We store our car's power in batteries. Are there batteries here?" Aidan asked, looking around.

Bert showed them a drawing of the workings of a typical hydroelectric dam and power plant. He pointed at the drawing.

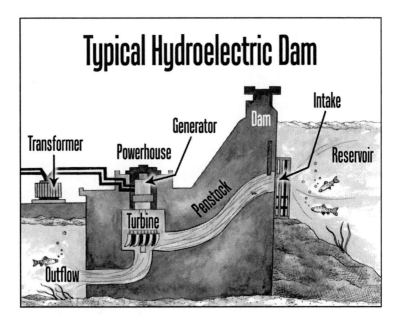

Typical Hydroelectric Dam

Transformer

Powerhouse

Generator

Dam

Intake

Reservoir

Penstock

Turbine

Outflow

"The water is stored in the reservoir just like your mom said. Gravity simply pulls it down through the water intake at the bottom of the dam wall. When it's allowed to go through, the water then turns the turbine, producing power. As for batteries, some power plants may have them, but the reservoir itself is a sort of battery. It stores the energy of the water until it's needed. There are gates that allow more or less water through depending on energy demands."

"We passed a lot of big smoke stacks on the drive through Utah to Wyoming," Nadia said. "Why doesn't this plant have big smoke stacks too?"

WYOMING

"The smoke from those smoke stacks is from the coal which was being burned there. Coal is another fossil fuel. When you don't use a fossil fuel, there isn't smoke pollution."

"Burning coal is really awful," Nadia said.

"We need to not think of it as awful, just outdated. We've learned a lot from using fossil fuels for energy. Back in its day, it was a step toward the future. We now need to concentrate on the transition from using fossil fuels toward our future where we don't use them at all. Yet, I'm grateful for all we learned to help us along the way."

Nadia thought about that for a while. She could see that Bert had a point.

Stephanie broke the silence. "How the electricity is produced at both types of power plants is similar, right?"

"Yes!" Bert answered. "Coal fired power plants and hydroelectric power plants both have turbines. The turbine rotates, or turns, just like an airplane's propeller. It even looks similar to an airplane's propeller. This propeller-looking-turbine turns the generator we saw. It's that generator, which is like a motor, which actually produces the electricity that is usable."

"So it's the falling water which turns the turbine for hydroelectricity?" Nadia asked.

"Yes," Bert answered.

"And how does burning coal turn the turbine?" Nadia asked.

"I bet it's the heat!" Aidan thought out loud, thinking of a hot air balloon soaring through the air.

"That's part of it. They use the heat to create steam with water in a boiler system. The steam pushes the turbine," Bert explained.

"How does the generator work?" Nadia asked.

"Well," Bert started, pointing at the drawing again. "The turbine converts the flowing water's energy into rotational energy. Then the generator converts that rotational energy into electrical energy."

"Sounds complicated," Nadia said, shaking her head.

"Yes, and no." Bert said with a smile. "The basic principles are pretty simple, but it gets a little complicated when you're dealing with something as large as a hydroelectric dam. In a large generator used at a plant like this, field poles are made from electromagnets with direct current. The field poles..."

"Does this have something to do with magnets and Faraday?" Aidan wondered. He loved playing with magnets and loved hearing about all the uses of magnets in the everyday world.

"Yes it does!"

"I think I've heard about this before," Aidan said, remembering the book that came in his magnet science kit.

WYOMING

"Okay, then I'll go a little more in depth," Bert agreed. "As Aidan already knows, a scientist named Michael Faraday did a lot of experiments with electricity and magnets. One of the things he found out was that when you move a magnet past a conductor, such as a copper wire, it causes electricity to flow through the wire. If you wind up the wire into a coil, you get even more electricity."

"So what exactly is electricity?" Nadia asked, trying to put it all together.

"For the purpose of what we've been talking about today, electricity is the movement or flow of electrically charged particles."

"Hmm," Nadia murmured.

"Now, for something as big as the generators in this dam, you need to use electromagnets. Regular, or 'permanent', magnets aren't strong enough or big enough. Electromagnets are made by putting coils of wire around iron. When you put electricity through the wire, the iron becomes magnetic. These electromagnets are mounted on the outside of the rotor and are called field poles because they have a magnetic *field* with a *pole*," Bert explained.

"Like the Earth has a north and south pole?" Aidan asked.

"Exactly, Aidan! The Earth is actually a great big magnet," Bert said.

Wright ✸n Time®

Aidan smiled thinking about the Earth as a giant magnet sticking to an even bigger refrigerator.

They understood about half of what Bert was saying, but didn't know what to ask, so they politely listened while they thought of questions to ask.

"The rotor turns around and around. As you can see by the drawing, it is attached to the shaft of the turbine. When it turns, it moves past mounted conductors—coils of wire. The turning causes electricity, or the flow of charged particles. The electricity is then sent out through transmission lines to be used in homes and businesses."

"Are these conductors anything like a train conductor?" Aidan asked.

"Or a symphony conductor?" Harrison asked.

"Not exactly, but sort of," Bert said. "These conductors aren't people, but all conductors tell other things where they are supposed to go. They all lead something important. Electrical conductors, basically wires, tell electricity where to go."

"Is there just one turbine in a hydroelectric plant?" Nadia asked, stuck on figuring out how the turbine worked.

"It depends on the plant. Some only have a few and some have a lot."

The concepts Bert was talking about were big, yet interesting. They continued walking around while the

WYOMING

Wrights asked question after question. Harrison took plenty of notes while they walked.

Nadia finally said, "I don't completely understand how this works. Can you simplify it a bit and explain it again?"

"For me, too," Harrison said, looking at the notes he was making for his article.

Nadia glanced at his notebook and noticed there were a lot of question marks all over the page.

"I'll start at the beginning again," Bert said as he tried to decide how best to explain it. "Basically, you have water flowing past a turbine. The turbine looks like big fan blades. So, the flowing water forces the blades to turn, just like a pinwheel in the wind. Got it so far?"

"Yes," Harrison said.

"Me, too," Nadia said.

"It's the next part that is the most interesting," Aidan said.

Stephanie smiled at her family and took a few photos of the group standing around talking.

"The turbine is connected by a shaft to a generator," he continued.

"This is where you lost me," Harrison said.

"Okay," Bert pointed to a second drawing of the turbine and generator. "A generator is like a big electric motor. Except, with a motor you put electricity in and you get spinning motion out. With a generator, you put in the spinning motion and get electricity out. They are inverses, or opposites, of each other. See?"

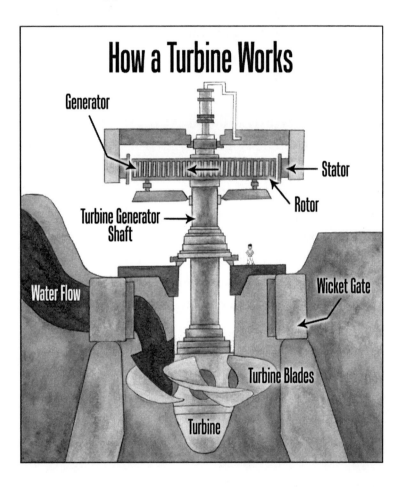

"Thanks!" Harrison said, looking at the diagram. "That helps make it a lot clearer." He pushed his glasses up and scribbled something in his notebook.

WYOMING

"But, how do you turn spinning into electricity?" Nadia asked.

"This is the cool part," Aidan whispered to his mother.

"This is where Faraday's discovery comes into play. Faraday discovered that if you spin a magnet inside a coil of wire, electricity starts flowing through that wire."

Bert looked at their faces to make sure they still understood him. Since they were all nodding, he continued.

"That's basically what is happening inside the generator. Our shaft is spinning magnets inside big coils of wire. In turn, we get electricity to come out! Isn't that great?"

The Wrights all nodded.

"I understood it this time!" Nadia said with glee.

"Yeah, those drawings really helped," Harrison said. "Do you think I could have copies of them for my article?"

"Sure, have these," Bert said. "I think those cover just about everything we've talked about. You asked some great questions. Let's go ahead to our next stop." Bert Hendricks had a surprise up his sleeve.

Once they got back into the car, Bert whispered to Harrison which direction to go. It was a short drive to the next spot and the children got excited as they got close. They were approaching an airport!

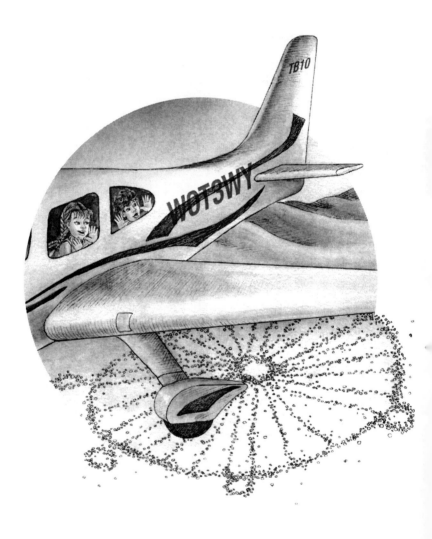

Chapter Six

"**A**re we going to be going on an airplane ride?" Aidan asked, full of excitement.

The seven year old boy loved going in all different types of transportation. He was keeping track of all the different types of vehicles he'd been on in his life. Cars and trucks were easy to mark off, then the RV, of course. He'd also been on a train once when he was a baby, an airplane twice, and a jet boat once. He couldn't wait for the day he got to ride in a semi-truck, a blimp, a helicopter, a barge, or on a cruise ship. He often wondered what other types of vehicles existed. As he thought about it, he remembered motorcycles and other adventurous vehicles like ATVs. He'd never been on any of those.

"Not only are we going to take a short airplane ride, but we're going to go in an experimental plane. My company helped design the engine. It uses a top-secret alternative energy for its power. It's extremely quiet and it can land like a helicopter."

"You mean it doesn't need a runway?" Nadia asked.

"Nope!" Bert answered with a big smile.

"Freaky awesome!" Aidan said.

"So which one is it?" Stephanie asked.

Bert pointed at a little red plane right near the building. This was a small private airport, so there weren't many airplanes in sight. "I've already filled out the flight plan. I just need to check in and then we can get going."

"Who's the pilot?" Nadia asked.

"I am," Bert said.

"Wow, you certainly are multi-talented!" Stephanie said.

"I've always felt it was important to follow *all* of my interests," he stated simply.

"I agree!" Stephanie quickly set her camera on a tripod and took a snapshot of the five of them in front of Bert's airplane. She set the timer again and took another shot of just the four Wrights for good measure.

WYOMING

Before they knew it, they were soaring through the air. The land lay out before them like a huge patchwork quilt. The cars and trains looked like toy cars on Disneyland's Peter Pan ride. The kids alternated between asking Bert questions about the plane and pointing out sites on the ground. They'd never had the opportunity to actually watch a pilot fly before. It was very exciting.

"This plane is shockingly quiet," Harrison told Bert. "I've never been on such a quiet airplane this size."

"Isn't it great?" Bert agreed. "It's so much fun to be able to hear my passengers without them screaming!" He chuckled loudly.

"Look at that river," Aidan exclaimed over the two men.

"Look at that cloud," Stephanie joined in. She was glad she'd put an extra memory card in her camera case. She'd already taken a couple hundred photographs that afternoon.

"We're about half way to our destination," Bert told his passengers. "Why don't you go ahead and have some dinner? Harrison, there should be a cooler right behind you. Will you get the food out for everyone?"

Harrison opened the cooler and passed sandwiches around.

"Peanut butter and jelly? My favorite!" Aidan exclaimed as he tore open the bag. He hadn't realized how hungry he had become.

Wright on Time

They all happily ate their sandwiches and blue corn tortilla chips. Bert had brought along apple juice and water to drink.

Half way through a bite of sandwich, Nadia exclaimed loudly, "Look! Look! Slow the plane down!"

They all looked down at the ground and saw a big spiral pictogram on the ground. It was a crop marking made by humans.

"There are a lot of crop circles and Native American ground drawings around this area," Bert said. "Some are even larger than that one, which looks similar to the Bighorn Medicine Wheel."

"I didn't know there were geoglyphs in Wyoming," Nadia said.

"I think they are just about everywhere," Harrison said.

"Really? Let's go see some more on our trip around the USA. This one looks so similar to the spiral on the Time Tuner. I wonder if there is one out there that is a perfect match."

"Time Tuner?" Bert asked.

"Yes, I meant to show it to you earlier!" Nadia got the device out of her bag and showed it to Bert. She told him all about finding it in a cave in Arizona, then discovering its special powers in Utah. He was especially impressed with its communication abilities. Nadia, on the other hand, was impressed with the way it glowed in the moonlight. She'd been spending hours every day scouring over the linguistic and metallurgic research their friend Maeve had sent.

"Maybe you can help us figure out what kind of alternative energy it is using to create the glow," Nadia said.

"It would be fantastic to find out what it is using to power itself," Bert said and became quiet again as he thought about this amazing device. "Wow! So, if you have your Time Tuner near you, you can be connected to the Internet no matter where you are?" Bert wanted clarification.

"That appears to be correct," Harrison said.

"The range is only about ten feet though, not as big as we'd like sometimes," Stephanie added. The Wright family had already gotten used to the device's Wi-Fi powers. They didn't seem extraordinarily special anymore.

"That's simply amazing," Bert said. "Try it here. I have a PDA in my bag."

"I have one too," Stephanie said. She got out her personal digital assistant and tried it. "Yep, works great. Best signal ever, in fact."

"Wow. I want one of those. I wonder who made it," Bert pondered. "There are a lot of secret projects going on right now, but I haven't even heard rumors of anything like that little device you have there."

Wright On Time

"I wish we knew who made it. We've spent quite a bit of time trying to figure that out," Stephanie said.

"We now are wondering if it's some top secret government equipment. Wherever it came from, we've been enjoying its mysteries," Harrison added.

"Yes… we have," Nadia added. "But, I still want to know why it has the turtle design similar to a crop circle on its back."

The plane and everyone on it were very quiet.

Chapter Seven

A short while later, Bert and the Wright family landed at the Wyoming Wind Project in southeastern Wyoming. The breeze had picked up compared to earlier in the day at Yellowstone. It was almost as if the wind knew the Wrights wanted to see a show.

As the Wrights and Bert Hendricks climbed out of the plane, Nadia quickly tucked her long braided hair into the hood of her sweatshirt while the rest put their hoods and hats on. The sun was nearly ready to set and it shone bright in their eyes, reminding them to put their sunglasses on.

Wright 🕳 n Time

"Thanks for the peanut butter and jelly sandwiches, Bert," Aidan said.

"No problem. I heard pb&j was your favorite meal," Bert replied.

"And, thanks for the hot sauce on mine," Harrison added. "That's my favorite condiment."

"Yeah, a little birdie told me that," he said with a laugh.

On the flight, Bert had told them they were going to the Foote Creek Rim in Wyoming. The terrain was completely different than at Yellowstone. They were on a large plateau and could see for miles in all directions.

Wind farm locations were chosen to be in areas where the wind was strong and the land was as flat and as desolate as possible. There was a little bit of scrub here and there, but mostly all the Wrights could see were rows and rows of giant white wind turbines. It was quite an impressive sight.

After a brief talk with the manager of the wind farm, Bert led the group around. They got into an electric golf cart and headed toward one of the turbines. The dirt path was well marked where visitors were allowed to go, and Bert followed it, pointing out specifics along the way.

"Unlike geysers, wind is found pretty much everywhere on earth," Bert said. "Harnessing that power is what a wind farm does. Much like a food farm, the product is gathered, collected, and distributed to customers."

WYOMING

As they got closer to the wind turbines the Time Tuner again glowed in Nadia's pocket where she had tucked it away.

"I can see why this place was chosen," Harrison said as he took notes.

"Yes, it's pretty obvious. No trees, elevated land, relatively level, and one of the windiest places in the U.S."

"Wow!" Stephanie said.

"It's freaky weird! It's like being in a strange white forest," Aidan commented. "How big are those freaky arm things?"

"The arms of a wind turbine are called rotors. They are big, aren't they? The diameter is forty-five meters. That's about, let's see," Bert did a quick calculation in his head, "one hundred and forty-seven and a half or so feet. I guess that'd be about forty or so Aidans."

Aidan gasped. "Forty of me? Freaky huge!"

"Yeah!" Nadia agreed. "But, how come they don't blow away?"

"Are they really secured in the ground? They seem kind of scary!" Stephanie said as she looked all around them feeling nervous about her family's safety.

Bert answered their questions. "The wind turbines are built to withstand very high winds. They can generate power when the wind is between eight and sixty-five miles per hour. Any gust stronger than that makes the turbine shut down. They are very secure in the ground. The towers are a tubular shape which makes them extremely stable and strong even in extremely high winds. They're not going anywhere, at least not today." He smiled reassuringly at Stephanie.

"How much power do they make?" Stephanie asked.

"Well, every single turbine you see here makes electricity for more than three-hundred and fifty houses. They also offset greenhouse gas emissions. Last I heard there are enough turbines at this wind farm to generate electricity for nearly thirteen-thousand houses."

"Three-hundred and fifty houses worth of power from each turbine?" Nadia asked.

"Wow, thirteen-thousand in total?" Stephanie asked.

"Yes. In fact, this wind farm even sends electricity to several other states. It's really a great project," Bert continued. "I've been working with some engineers to try and find a way to store wind energy in vehicles. It's got a long ways to go, but it's important we never limit our options. There are so many possibilities. The permanent replacements for fossil fuels could be right in front of our faces!"

When they got close to a turbine, Bert stopped the golf cart and they all hopped off. As they walked closer to it, the wind picked up even more and sprinkles of rain

WYOMING

started to spit in their faces, making it hard for them to concentrate on the turbines.

As they neared the turbine, Aidan pointed out a cow grazing on the scrub.

"Nearly all the land here can still be grazed by animals," Bert told him.

The cow reminded Nadia of a question she'd thought of earlier. "I heard that animals are harmed by wind farms, especially birds. Is that true?" Nadia said.

The wind was picking up and Bert had to raise his voice in order to be heard. "Animal welfare is definitely an important issue. There have been special task forces which have come up with ways to minimize the harm to animals. Some ideas are working really well and they are always looking for more ideas."

"What ideas are they using now?" Nadia asked.

"Part of the design for tubular wind towers, like the ones here, includes all the cables being buried underground. This makes it so birds don't have a place to perch. So the area isn't attractive for birds to nest. There are also no turbines in the areas where birds live now, like the edge of the plateau rim."

"Won't they fly into the blades?" Aidan wondered.

"They could, that's true. But, the blades move really slowly and they are coated with a special ultraviolet reflective paint which helps the birds see the blades. This alone has stopped the birds from flying into the blades. There are people who keep track of how many birds are harmed by the turbines and they help think of new ways to prevent it."

"Mom, I'm cold," Aidan said. "Can we go back soon?"

As if on cue, a few raindrops sprinkled in Stephanie's mouth as she tried to answer Aidan. She took his hand and started to walk around the turbine while Bert showed Harrison a few last details for his article.

Oh no, please don't rain... not now, Nadia thought to herself.

Chapter Eight

S uddenly, the sprinkles turned into a downpour. The sheets of rain pouring down made Nadia worry about the Time Tuner. She'd put it in the windbreaker pocket, hoping to keep it safe. But, the jacket wasn't waterproof. The tag had said *water resistant*. The rain could still come through her pocket. Based on the metallurgist's earlier e-mail, she still hadn't determined what the device was made of, and Nadia was worried it was a metal which would rust.

Wright on Time®

Stephanie ran through the pouring rain, trying to get to the covered golf cart as quickly as possible. Everyone's hair and clothing were drenched.

Aidan lagged behind. He stomped his feet in the dirt as it quickly turned into mud. The more he stomped, the more the mud spread. The squishing squelch of mud made a fabulous noise. Aidan happily stopped where he was and started pounding his feet, one at a time. Being from southern Arizona, he hadn't had much opportunity to play in rain before, so he was enjoying it despite the cold.

Harrison and Nadia were running as fast as they could. Harrison's wet and dark sunglasses were making it hard for him to see. His regular eyeglasses were left in the airplane. Since the sunglasses were prescription, he didn't want to take them off. He couldn't see anything without them.

Stephanie hollered for Aidan to follow her over the noise of the downpour. Since he wasn't following, and she didn't want to wait for him to catch up with her, she went back to him. The boy's legs were plastered in mud almost to his hips, and there were speckles of mud on his face, accenting his enormous smile. Stephanie briefly wondered how she was going to get all the mud off of him, when all of a sudden she heard a scream.

WYOMING

"Ahhhhhh," the scream continued. The rain was coming down so hard and so loud it was difficult to tell who was making the sound. Finally, Stephanie recognized the voice. It was her husband, Harrison.

"Harrison, are you all right?" Stephanie called toward the golf cart. She couldn't see anything with the rain and the drops in her eyes.

Harrison was always the calm one, so she was getting really worried and Aidan could see it.

"Aidan, come." She grabbed her son's muddy hand and they ran together toward the golf cart.

They quickly found Harrison, sitting smack dab in the mud. He was rubbing his foot. He saw the concern on Stephanie's face.

"Are you okay?" Stephanie tried to say calmly.

"I'm fine. I'm fine," Harrison said. He smiled up at his family, wiping the rain and mud from his face, looking abashed. "Sorry my scream worried you, honey."

"Dad tripped over that root," Nadia said as she pointed toward a gnarly root system.

Harrison took off his glasses and wiped them with the inside of his long sleeved shirt. He was glad he'd changed out of the greasy one from earlier when he'd been working on the RV engine, but he was afraid he might have ruined two shirts in one day. The mud was everywhere.

Wright🪲n Time®

"Roots?" Bert asked as he joined the family and looked around. "That's odd... and very unusual for this area. I've never seen deep roots like that before."

"Well, they're here now," Harrison laughed.

"And they're *moving!*" Aidan announced, with fear in his voice. He started to back up slowly.

"Oh, it's just the strong wind," Harrison said.

"Oh, no it's not!" Stephanie made a little yelp and pulled Aidan quickly away from the root system.

Bert was leaning over, looking at the roots, when a stalk popped out of the top. Whatever it was, it was growing at a very quick rate. He touched the plant and said something to himself no one else could hear, even though the rain had died down to a drizzle again.

"Oh, no," Nadia cried and everyone turned to look at her. She held out the Time Tuner.

"It has mud and rain on it! I think it's ruined."

"Here, let me see it." Harrison took the device and immediately a different set of roots began to form on the ground near his hand. He was oblivious to the growth as he wiped off the device just as he'd previously wiped off his eyeglasses.

The device had turned a dim green. It appeared to have a slight glow from the inside, but it was hard to tell in the bright setting sunlight. The rain completely stopped

WYOMING

where they were standing and a double rainbow popped up in the distance.

"Look at this," Harrison motioned for everyone to look at the device. "I don't think it's ruined, but it has turned green and there seem to be new symbols on it!"

Nadia touched one. "That one looks very similar to the crop circles we just flew over." A droplet of water rolled down Nadia's finger. It landed on the device. Immediately, a glowing blue spread over it wiping out all the images that were on it. Once the blue covered the entire device, a new bright white symbol appeared. Nadia tried to imprint the glyph in her memory, as the green glyph was already fading from her mind.

Harrison and Nadia alternated holding up the device and examining it from all angles. The blue quickly faded and the whole thing turned back to the original black and bronze again.

"What just happened?" Nadia asked as she passed the Time Tuner to her dad, incredulous.

"I have no idea," Harrison replied. He unintentionally set his hand on the muddy ground again and brought a bit of the mud with him when he touched the device. It immediately turned green again.

Harrison and Nadia looked at each other and then back at the device again.

"Oh, my!" Bert hollered. "It's growing again."

Wright ✦n Time®

Stephanie's attention was caught and she grabbed Nadia's hand, pulling her away from where the two root systems were growing. It looked like time-lapse photography in action.

Harrison backed away as the plants grew closer and closer to him until he was almost lying flat on his back. One vine stretched up near his face and then, with a gentle *pop*, it produced a bunch of grapes!

Harrison breathed a sigh of relief and started to pick himself up from the ground. Before he had stood all the way up, a grape vine and a sunflower had fully formed in between him and Bert. The two men stood and admired the plants. They'd completely stopped growing and were stretching their leaves toward the setting sun. Bert gently touched one.

"I think it's safe," Harrison said to Stephanie. With his reassurance, she brought the children closer.

"How strange," Nadia said. "I was just thinking about sunflowers."

"And I was just thinking about grapes," added Harrison.

"Dad, do you think the Time Tuner did this?" Nadia asked, still amazed.

"I can't think what else could have caused something like this."

"May I see the Time Tuner again?" Bert asked.

Harrison held out the device to Bert. When Bert took the device, it was black and bronze again. Bert

WYOMING

purposefully put a dab of mud on it to see what would happen. On cue, it turned green again and another plant sprouted up right next to Bert.

"Carrot," Bert said, before the plant had even fully formed. "I've been hungry for carrots all day."

Stephanie pulled at the green plant once it had stopped growing and out popped a carrot. She stood there dumbfounded.

Bert took the carrot from her and took a bite off the end. "It's good," he nodded approvingly. "Yep, it hits the spot," he said as he ate the rest of the carrot.

Stephanie and Aidan both tried holding the device and putting a drop of mud on it. Stephanie produced a strawberry plant and Aidan's thoughts produced corn. The plants grew until their produce was ripe and then stopped.

"Freaky cool," Aidan said. He couldn't think of any more words to say.

Neither could any of the adults. *Freaky* and *cool* were the perfect words for what the Time Tuner could do. They stood there in silence looking at their plants.

It was Nadia who broke the silence. She couldn't help it. The magnitude of what had happened in the mud was too much for her to stop the words from coming out of her mouth.

"What *is this thing*?" she asked.

But, no one answered.

Chapter Nine

In the airplane, Nadia got out her notebook and took notes about their day. What had started out as a slow and simple day had turned into a day that was anything but slow or simple. The Time Tuner had so many new powers, it was overwhelming.

Aidan stared out the plane's window, trying to see the ground. The clouds and new moon made the sky extremely dark. There wasn't a star that could be seen. He was looking at the device and pressing on it, trying to get it to do something. He kept holding it up to the window trying to get the moonlight to make it glow like it had in Utah, but it never did.

"Do you think we could get it to make doughnut trees?" Aidan asked.

"I don't think so," Nadia answered.

"Well it wouldn't hurt to try," Aidan said, licking his lips just thinking about it.

"No, it wouldn't," Nadia said, thinking about all the things she was wanted to try and get the Time Tuner to grow.

The flight was short, yet the children both fell asleep during the quiet flight back to their car. Harrison carried Nadia to their car and Stephanie carried Aidan. They loved carrying the kids. They knew it was only a short time in their lives they'd be able to and Stephanie already couldn't pick up Nadia anymore.

As they approached their campground, the children woke up.

"Now kids," Stephanie said. "I left some clothes and shampoo in the shower room lockers at the campground. I thought we'd all get out of these muddy, wet clothes and shower and change before we head to our RV for the night."

Nadia and Aidan were cold and tired of being wet, so they quickly agreed as they began to shiver.

WYOMING

It was weird talking about ordinary things when it had been such an extraordinary day. Yet the idea of a hot shower and clean dry clothes sounded wonderful, even to Aidan, who normally hated taking the time to get clean. He stifled a yawn as he went with his dad into the men's shower room.

THE WRIGHT FAMILY'S LATEST PORTRAIT

Chapter Ten

On the short walk from the showers to the RV, Harrison handed both Nadia and Aidan business cards from Bert. Bert had written notes on the back of each.

The message to Nadia said:

> "It was so awesome meeting you today. E-mail or call me anytime if you ever want to talk about the Time Tuner. Keep it safe. Have a great trip! Fondly, Bert"

Wright on Time

The message to Aidan said:

> "You're a freaky cool kid! I can't wait to shoot some hoops with you sometime. Be sure to let me know the next time you are in my neighborhood. Your friend, Bert"

"Wow! He gave me his autograph," Aidan said. He then rushed through the door of their RV and hollered, "Prince Pumpkin the Third! We're *home*!"

"Yes," Nadia collapsed on the kitchen bench right next to the turtle's terrarium. She smiled at the little turtle as she held onto the Time Tuner tightly in her hand.

Prince Pumpkin III lifted his head and nodded at Nadia before turning his head to look at Aidan. Aidan reached down and rubbed the top of the turtle's little head.

"We are most definitely, positively, absolutely, resolutely and every other –ly word in the whole wide world, *home*. I love our home," Nadia said.

Stephanie and Harrison smiled at each other. With everything that had happened that day and everything they didn't understand, it felt wonderful to know they were all home in their RV... together.

THE END

GLOSSARY

algae [**al**-gee]; a plant-like organism which grows in water

Allosaurus fragilis [ahl-oh-**sohr**-uhs] [**fra**-jil-uhs]; Utah's state dinosaur. It was a large and smart carnivore that lived in the late Jurassic period and walked on two legs. Up to 16.5 feet tall, 38 feet long, and 1400 kilograms.

archeology [ahr-kee-**ahl**-*uh*-jee]; careful study of past human life and cultures by examining found evidence.

Wright 🕱n Time®

Bighorn Medicine Wheel; manmade land form in the shape of a large circle with 28 spokes, like a wheel. About 700 years old, 80 feet in diameter and 245 feet in circumference. Located in north-central Wyoming.

biodiesel [bahy-oh-**dee**-z*uh*l]; special fuel designed for a diesel engine.

biomass [**bahy**-oh-mas]; organic matter that can be converted to fuel. Examples include wood, plant waste, and garbage.

caldera [kal-**der**-*uh*]; bowl shaped depression from an explosion or a collapse of a volcano.

carbon [**kahr**-b*uh*n]; element that occurs in all organic objects.

carbon dioxide [**kahr**-b*uh*n] [dahy-**ok**-sahyd]; a gas made from one part carbon and two parts oxygen.

carbon monoxide [**kahr**-b*uh*n] [m*uh*-**nok**-sahyd]; a gas made from one part carbon and one part oxygen.

WYOMING

condiment [**kon**-d*uh*-ment]; ingredient added to food after it has been cooked. Examples include Tabasco sauce, ketchup, salt, pepper, and mustard.

conductor [k*uh*n-**duhk**-ter]; device or substance which allows electricity to flow through it.

crater [**krey**-ter]; circle shaped hole in the ground formed from a large rock, or meteorite, which fell from space.

cryptogram [**krip**-t*uh*-gram]; secret writing in a code or cipher.

debug [dee-**buhg**]; to detect and remove errors from (a computer program). *Stephanie Wright debugged her computer program.*

decipher [dee-**sie**-fer]; to discover the meaning of an object. *Nadia helped decipher the strange markings on the Time Tuner.*

dumbfounded [**duhm**-found-ed]; amazed into silence.

electricity [ee-lek-**tris**-i-tee]; the flow of electrons and their charge.

Wright 🐢n Time®

electromagnet [ee-lek-troh-**mag**-nit]; device which contains a magnetized core with wires wrapped around it. Electricity runs through the wires, producing the magnetism.

engineer [en-j*uh*-**neer**]; specially trained person who runs a machine or designs something in particular.

Faraday [**fair**-*uh*-dey]; Michael Faraday, 1791-1867, talented English chemist and physicist who did many experiments with electricity and magnetism.

finagling [fi-**ney**-*guh*-ling]; to trick or manipulate, often in a playful way.

Foote Creek Rim; plateau area located in southeastern Wyoming.

Four corners; spot where four states meet at one point. The four states are Arizona, Utah, Colorado and New Mexico.

freaky awesome, freaky cool, freaky weird, freaky wow; fun phrases Aidan Wright is popularizing. *Aidan saw a really neat object. "Freaky cool!" he said.*

WYOMING

freelance writer; the job of a writer who works alone and is contracted for specific writing assignments. *Harrison Wright is a freelance writer.*

fumarole [**fyoo**-m*uh*-rohl]; hole in or near a volcano, especially an old one, where vapor rises.

furcula [**fur**-ky*uh*-l*uh*]; wish bone, the forked collar bone of a bird or dinosaur. *The Allosaurus fragilis has a furcula. Aidan helped uncover one in Utah.*

furrow [**fuhr**-*oh*]; to wrinkle up your face.

generator [**jen**-*uh*-rey-ter]; machine which converts one type of energy into another.

geoglyph [**gee**-oh-glif]; glyph written on the ground which can be seen best from an aerial view. *The Wrights saw pictures on the ground when they were flying in an airplane. Those pictures were geoglyphs.*

geothermal [gee-oh-**thur**-m*uh*l]; internal heat of the earth.

geyser [**gahy**-zer]; jets of water and steam which spout up from a hot spring.

Wright ✺n Time®

glyph [glif]; pictograph or hieroglyph.

hieroglyph [hie-ro-**glif**]; having to do with a symbol which is a picture that represents a word or sound.

homeschooled [**hohm**-skoold]; educated at home. *The Wright children are homeschooled.*

hot springs; a spring of hot water which is geothermally heated.

hydrocarbon [**hy**-dro-kahr-b*uh*n]; organic compound made of hydrogen and carbon, often used as a fuel.

hydroelectric power plant; plant where electricity is generated from the flowing of water.

hydrothermal [hy-dro-**thur**-m*uh*l]; pertaining to a hot liquid.

incredulous [in-**kred**-u-l*uhs*]; amazed and hardly believing.

inverse [in-**vurs**]; opposites.

linguistics [ling-**gwis**-tiks]; the science of languages.

WYOMING

mechanic [m*uh*-**kan**-ik]; person who maintains and repairs machinery and motors.

mechanical [m*uh*-**kan**-i-k*uh*l]; having to do with machinery.

metallurgist [**met**-ah-lur-jist]; person who works with metals.

mudpot; hot spring or fumarole with a pool of bubbling mud.

oil derrick [*oy*l] [**der**-ik]; tower framework over an oil well.

organic matter; material made from things which are living or were living.

origami [or-ih-**gah**-mee]; Japanese art of folding paper into decorative shapes.

paleontology [pey-lee-*uh*n-**tahl**-*uh*-jee]; study of life existing in former geological periods, using fossils.

patent [**pat**-nt]; the right to use, market, and sell an invention when no one else is allowed to, granted by a

Wright ✹n Time®

government. *Some of the secret alternate fuel ideas that Bert talked about were patented. Inventors get patents on their inventions so that they own them.*

petroleum [p*uh*-**troh**-lee-*uh*m]; a special liquid used as fuel.

pictograph [**pik**-t*uh*-graf]; a picture or symbol that represents a word.

pictogram [**pik**-t*uh*-gram]; See pictograph.

plateau [pla-**toh**]; a raised area of land that is flat.

prehistoric [pree-hi-**stor**-ik]; before written history, like when dinosaurs roamed the earth.

prismatic [priz-**mat**-ik]; brilliantly colored, formed by refraction of light.

propeller [pr*o*-**pel**-er]; radiating blades on a rotating shaft. *Airplanes and boats have propellers.*

prototype [**proh**-toh-tahyp]; the original design of something.

WYOMING

proximity [prok-**sim**-i-tee]; how close two objects are to each other.

shaft [shahft]; a pole. *The turbine had a large metal shaft which rotated.*

recreational vehicle (RV); large vehicle that people can travel and live in. *The Wright family live in an RV.*

renewable [ree-**noo**-a-bul]; something that can be recreated in a short period of time.

reservoir [**rez**-*uh*-vwahr]; a place where water is collected and stored.

revolution [rev-*uh*-**loo**-sh*uh*n]; the orbiting of one object around another.

rotor [**roh**-ter]; rotating part of a machine.

telecommute [**tel**-i-k*uh*-myoot]; to work at home or on the road using a computer that is connected to a company's network.

terrain [**ter**-eyn]; what the land is like in a particular area.

Wright ✦n Time®

terrarium [ter-**rair**-ee-*uh*m]; a glass or plastic container for a small land animal and/or plants to live in.

Time Tuner; amazing device the Wright family found in a salted cave in Southern Arizona, properties currently unknown.

tributary [**trih**-byoo-tair-ee]; a river or stream which flows into a larger river.

turbine [**tur**-bahyn]; machine with a rotor which helps produce electricity.

ultraviolet [uhl-tr*uh*-**vahy**-*uh*-lit]; beyond the violet in the light wave spectrum.

vernacular [ver-**nak**-y*uh*-ler]; a style of language which is specific to a place or group of people. *Aidan Wright has a particular vernacular that includes the word 'freaky' frequently.*

VoIP, Voice over Internet Protocol; computer program that lets you talk to someone else over your computer as though you were using a telephone.

voltage [**vohl**-tij]; the amount of force pushing electricity through a circuit.

WYOMING

water vole [**wah**-ter] [vohl]; mouse-like rodent with a short tail.

Wyoming Wind Project; wind farm in southeastern Wyoming.

Yellowstone National Park; National Park famous for its geysers located in Wyoming, Idaho and Montana.

zooplankton [zoh-*uh*-**plangk**-tuhn]; really small animal-like masses which live in water.

Wright 🐢n Time®

MORE FACTS ABOUT WYOMING

- Highest Point: Gannett Peak, 13,802 feet above sea level.
- Lowest Point: Belle Fourche River at 3099 feet above sea level.
- Size: 97,814 square miles (10th largest state).
- Residents are called: Wyomingites.
- 44th state to officially become a state.
- Average Precipitation: 14.5 inches per year.
- Largest Lake: Yellowstone Lake.
- Bordering States: Colorado, Montana, Nebraska, South Dakota, Utah, Idaho.
- First state to give women the right to vote.
- State Butterfly: Sheridan's Green Hairstreak.
- State Coin: Sacajawea Golden Dollar.
- State Dinosaur: Triceratops.
- State Grass: Western Wheatgrass.
- State Meaning: Large Prairie Place.
- State Motto: "Equal Rights".
- State Soil: Forkwood soil.
- State Sport: Rodeo.

**What is the image the Wright family sees on the
*Time Tuner?***

In Arizona, the Wright family found a *mysterious*
device which shows an image of a turtle with a special
symbol in the middle. The symbol is based off of an
ancient Mayan glyph called a **Hunab Ku** symbol. The
Mayans believed that the symbol represented the gateway
to other galaxies beyond our own sun. Only the maker
of the device understands why the Hunab Ku was drawn
inside of a turtle on the *Time Tuner*. Check out **www.
WrightOnTimeBooks.com** and read *Wright on Time:
SOUTH DAKOTA, Book 4* to find out more!

Dear Readers,

I hope you've enjoyed this book about my family. I've started my very own blog, telling all about places we've been and things we've seen that aren't in these books. I can't tell you where we are right now since that's top secret, but there are sure to be places that we've been that you'll find interesting.

To read more, and to tell me of places my family and I should check out (I love comments), see my blog at **www. WrightOnTimeBooks.com/nadia**. Aidan says he thinks it's freaky cool!

Love,
Nadia

Join Nadia and Aidan on their first adventure in *Wright on Time: ARIZONA, Book 1*. There the Wrights explored a salted cave. Nadia hoped to find minerals and see rock formations. Aidan really wanted to see bats. This is the adventure where the mysterious device was found. Where was it, and what does it do? Published in August 2009.

Join Nadia and Aidan as they continue their adventures in *Wright on Time: UTAH, Book 2*. The Wrights have joined a dinosaur dig searching for allosaurus bones. Will they find any and what will they learn about that mysterious device? Published in November 2009.

Join Nadia and Aidan as they continue their adventures in *Wright on Time: SOUTH DAKOTA, Book 4* coming out in Fall 2010. The Wrights visit the Black Hills, the Sturgis motorcycle rally and a newspaper, and get to play with the Time Tuner. Be sure to check out **www.WrightOnTimeBooks.com** for even more fun and games, and a forum for you to post your own adventure tips!

A Journey Through Learning

Children absorb information by using their hands. Put a lapbook into your child's hands and watch the learning begin!

A lapbook is a series of file folders glued together and loaded inside with mini-booklets. Your child records the information he/she learns inside the mini-booklets.

We carry lapbooks for all the Wright on Time books. We also have lapbooks for history, science, bible, math, literature, seasons, holidays, and early learning. Please visit our website at www.ajourneythroughlearning.com.

Tanja Bauerle at age 11 with her dog, Swift. Swift never barked and he could climb trees!

Tanja was a busy girl growing up. Born in Germany, she moved to Australia when she was 11, and later to the USA as an adult. Her favorite childhood activities were drawing and coloring. Her love for animated movies inspired her to pursue a degree in animation. Illustrators like Graeme Base and Arthur Rackham inspired to her pursue her illustrating dreams!

Check out www.TanjaBauerle.com for more information about Tanja and her award winning work.

Lisa Cottrell-Bentley at age 9.5 with her favorite puzzle collection.

Lisa was born in Iowa and raised in Illinois and Iowa. She moved to Arizona as an adult. Her favorite childhood activities were writing, solving puzzles of all kinds, and dreaming up stories and creative inventions. Her love of number puzzles inspired her to pursue a degree in mathematics. Children's book authors like Beverly Cleary and Meg Cabot inspired her to pursue her writing dreams!

Check out www.WrightOnTimeBooks.com for more information about Lisa and her children's chapter book series.

NOTES:

NOTES:

Wright **☀n** Time®

Flat Aidan

Color Aidan, cut him out and take him with you.

Color Nadia, cut her out and take her with you.

CPSIA information can be obtained at www.ICGtesting.com
Printed in the USA
LVOW10s2122140515

438611LV00001B/19/P